For Thomas—HNC   For Jim and the cows—RB

Macmillan Publishing Company, 866 Third Avenue, New York, NY 10022. Maxwell Macmillan Canada, Inc., 1200 Eglinton Avenue East, Suite 200, Don Mills, Ontario M3C 3N1. Macmillan Publishing Company is part of the Maxwell Communication Group of Companies. First American edition. Printed and bound in Hong Kong by South China Printing Company (1988) Ltd. 10 9 8 7 6 5 4 3 2 1   Book design by Julie Quan.

Library of Congress Cataloging-in-Publication Data. Coulter, Hope Norman, date. Uncle Chuck's truck / by Hope Norman Coulter ; illustrations by Rick Brown. — 1st American ed.   p.   cm.   Summary: When Uncle Chuck's truck gets stuck in the mud while he is taking food to the cows on his farm, the cows come to the rescue. ISBN 0-02-724825-9 [1. Trucks—Fiction. 2. Cows—Fiction. 3. Farm life—Fiction. 4. Uncles—Fiction.] I. Brown, Rick, date. ill. II. Title.   PZ7. C83075Un   1993 [E]—dc20   91-42638

Uncle Chuck's Truck

by Hope Norman Coulter   illustrations by Rick Brown

Bradbury Press   New York

Maxwell Macmillan Canada   Toronto
Maxwell Macmillan International
New York   Oxford   Singapore   Sydney

My Uncle Chuck drives a truck on his farm.

I love to ride in it with him.

We go bouncing, bouncing, bouncing
over the bumps where his farm is bumpy,

and sliding, sliding, sliding over the
slippery mud where his farm is muddy.

Uncle Chuck puts different things in the back of his truck. In the winter he puts food for his cows back there.

I go with him—bounce, bounce, bounce,
slip-slide, slip-slide, slip-slide—

riding back to take care of the cows.

When the cows see Uncle Chuck's
truck, they say MOO and start
running toward us.

They're ready to eat!

Uncle Chuck puts their food on the ground.

We count the cows. "Any new baby cows?"

"Yes, there's one that was born during the night."

Now it's time to go.
Br-rm-rm-rm-rm. The truck won't go.
We're stuck!

Uncle Chuck's truck is stuck in the mud!
"Oh, brother," says Uncle Chuck.

So four cows put their heads behind
the truck and push hard. The truck comes
unstuck from the mud, and away we go.

"All right!" says Uncle Chuck.
"Thanks, cows! See you tomorrow."